MW01099050

Presented to

_____

Date

_____

Kids-Life™

Easter Storybook

Mary Hollingsworth

**Illustrated by
Rick Incrocci**

Chariot Books™
A Division of Cook Communications

Kids-Life Easter Storybook

©1995 by Educational Publishing Concepts, Inc., Wheaton, IL
Exclusive Distribution by Chariot Family Publishing

Printed in The United States of America.
7 6 5 4 3 2 1   99 98 97 96 95

Table of Contents

Dear Parents,

The Easter story is the most important story in the Bible. It provides the key to open our understanding of God's love for us, as well as shows us how He made provision for our salvation.

The four stories in this book present the events of Easter in a way that your child will love and understand. The stories tell the facts, and, at the same time, help your child understand the depths of God's love for him or her.

You will want to read this book over and over again as you share with your child the greatest love story ever known, God's love for His children.

The Editors

The Last Supper

Luke 22:7-20; I Corinthians 11:23-26

Every year God's people ate the Passover meal. The meal helped them remember how God had saved them from slavery in Egypt. Jesus had asked Peter and John to get the Passover meal ready. They would eat it together in an upstairs room.

When the meal was ready, Jesus and His helpers sat down. Jesus said, "I wanted to eat this Passover meal with you before I die. The next time we eat it, we will be in the kingdom of God. Then it will have even more meaning."

Jesus took some bread. He thanked God for it and gave it to His helpers. He said, "This bread will remind you of My body. Think of Me when you eat it."

Then Jesus took a cup of wine. He gave thanks to God for it. He said, "This cup shows the new agreement from God to His people. The new agreement will begin when I die. This wine will remind you of My blood. When you drink the wine, do it to remember Me." After the supper, they sang a song and left.

Now, every time we eat the bread and drink the wine, we remember Jesus. And we show other people about His death. We will keep on doing this until Jesus comes again.

Kids-Life™ QUESTIONS

1. What was the Passover meal supposed to remind God's people of?

2. What was the Passover meal?

3. Where did Jesus and His helpers eat the Passover meal?

4. Jesus said the bread and wine should remind us of something. What?

FUN & FACTS

During the Passover meal each Jewish family sang songs. These songs praised God and thanked Him for saving them from slavery. You can read the words to the songs they sang: Psalms 113, 114, 115, 116, 117, 118, and 136. Maybe you can make up a tune to one of these songs and sing it.

Soldiers Arrest Jesus

Mark 14:32-50

After the Last Supper, Jesus and His helpers went to the Mount of Olives. This was a mountain where many olive trees grew. Jesus went off by Himself and prayed three diffferent times. His helpers fell asleep.

Jesus came back and said, "Get up! We must go. Here comes the man who will give Me to My enemies." *Tromp, tromp, tromp*! At that moment Judas Iscariot brought a group of soldiers and other people to Jesus. Judas had been one of Jesus' helpers.

These people were sent by the leading priests, teachers of God's law, and the older Jewish leaders. They all had swords and clubs! Judas had told the soldiers to watch for his signal. He would kiss the man who was Jesus.

Judas came up to Jesus and said, "Teacher!" He kissed Jesus. Then the men grabbed Jesus and arrested Him.

Jesus said, "These things have happened to make the Scriptures come true." Then all of Jesus' helpers left Him and ran away.

Kids-Life™ QUESTIONS

1. Who gave Jesus to His enemies?

2. Why did Judas kiss Jesus?

3. Why do you think Jesus' helpers ran away?

4. Did you ever run away from something you were afraid of? Why?

FUN & FACTS

Judas was an evil man. He had taken care of the money for Jesus and His helpers. But he had stolen some of it for himself. In this part of the story, he sells Jesus to His enemies for 30 silver coins. For that little bit of money, Judas sold the Son of God.

Jesus Dies

Matthew 27:32-61; Mark 15:16-47

Jesus was put on trial. Because people lied about Him to the judge, Jesus was found guilty. They said He had to die on a cross.

On Friday, the soldiers beat Jesus. He was very weak. He could not carry the heavy wooden cross to the place where they would crucify Him. The soldiers made a man named Simon carry the cross for Jesus.

The soldiers led Jesus to a place called
Golgotha. It was a hill outside of
Jerusalem. There they nailed Jesus to the
cross. Then the soldiers gambled for Jesus'
clothes. It was nine o'clock in the morning.

A sign was nailed to Jesus' cross. It said, "The King of the Jews." Two robbers were nailed to crosses, too. People walked by and said ugly things to Jesus. "Save Yourself! Come down from the cross, if You are the Son of God!"

At noon, the whole country became dark. The darkness lasted for three hours. At three o'clock, Jesus died for the sins of the world.

When Jesus died, the huge curtain in the temple split into two pieces. It ripped from top to bottom! The earth shook, and rocks broke apart! Graves opened, and dead people came back to life. The soldiers guarding Jesus said, "He really was the Son of God!"

On Friday evening, Jesus was buried. A man named Joseph buried Him in his own new tomb. A huge stone was put in front of the opening. Jesus was dead, and His followers were very sad.

Kids-Life™ QUESTIONS

1. Who made the earth get dark when Jesus was dying?

2. Who buried Jesus?

3. On what day of the week did Jesus die?

4. How do you feel when you think about Jesus dying on the cross?

FUN & FACTS

The curtain that tore in two when Jesus died was very special. It was woven of blue, purple, and scarlet yarn and finely twisted linen cloth. On it were sewn wonderful pictures of cherubim (angels). The curtain was fifteen feet high and about four inches thick! So, it did not tear by itself—God had to do it.

Jesus Lives Again

Matthew 28:1-10

Early Sunday morning two women went to look at Jesus' grave. They were Mary Magdalene and another woman named Mary.

At that time there was a strong earthquake! An angel of the Lord came down from heaven. *Rumble, rumble.* He rolled the stone away from Jesus' tomb. He was shining as bright as a flash of lightning. His clothes were as white as new snow.

The soldiers guarding the tomb were very frightened of the angel. They shook with fear. Then they became as still as dead men.

The angel said to the two women, "Don't be afraid. I know that you are looking for Jesus who died. He is not here. He has come back to life! It's just as He said it would be. Go quickly and tell His followers that He is alive!"

The women were afraid, but they were so happy! They ran to tell Jesus' followers what had happened. As they were going, Jesus met them. They bowed down, held on to Jesus' feet, and worshipped Him. Jesus said, "Don't be afraid. Go and tell My helpers to go to Galilee. They will see Me there."

The two women ran to tell Jesus' helpers that He was alive. The eleven helpers went to Galilee. They went to the mountain where Jesus told them to go. On the mountain they saw Jesus and worshipped Him. Jesus was alive again!

Kids-Life™ QUESTIONS

1. Who were the two women at Jesus' tomb on Sunday morning?

2. What did the angel say?

3. Why were the two Marys so happy?

4. How can Jesus help us because He's alive today?

FUN & FACTS

The word *angel* is a Greek word that means *messenger.* Angels are beings from heaven. They can sometimes look like people. God used angels to help His people and to announce important events. Angels announced the birth of Jesus to the shepherds. Now, they were announcing that Jesus had risen from the dead!